to-Read Book

p for
Dear Dragon

by Margaret Hillert
Illustrated by Jack Pullan

NORWOOD HOUSE PRESS

DEAR CAREGIVER,

The books in this Beginning-to-Read collection may look somewhat familiar in that the original versions could have been a part of your own early reading experiences. These carefully written texts feature common sight words to provide your child multiple exposures to the words appearing most frequently in written text. These new versions have been updated and the engaging illustrations are highly appealing to a contemporary audience of young readers.

Begin by reading the story to your child, followed by letting him or her read familiar words and soon your child will be able to read the story independently. At each step of the way, be sure to praise your reader's efforts to build his or her confidence as an independent reader. Discuss the pictures and encourage your child to make connections between the story and his or her own life. At the end of the story, you will find reading activities and a word list that will help your child practice and strengthen beginning reading skills. These activities, along with the comprehension questions are aligned to current standards, so reading efforts at home will directly support the instructional goals in the classroom.

Above all, the most important part of the reading experience is to have fun and enjoy it!

Shannon Cannon

Shannon Cannon,
Literacy Consultant

Norwood House Press • www.norwoodhousepress.com
Beginning-to-Read™ is a registered trademark of Norwood House Press.
Illustration and cover design copyright ©2017 by Norwood House Press. All Rights Reserved.

Authorized adapted reprint from the U.S. English language edition, entitled Help for Dear Dragon by Margaret Hillert. Copyright © 2017 Margaret Hillert. Reprinted with permission. All rights reserved. Pearson and Help for Dear Dragon are trademarks, in the US and/or other countries, of Pearson Education, Inc. or its affiliates. This publication is protected by copyright, and prior permission to re-use in any way in any format is required by both Norwood House Press and Pearson Education. This book is authorized in the United States for use in schools and public libraries.

LIBRARY OF CONGRESS CATALOGING-IN-PUBLICATION DATA

Names: Hillert, Margaret, author. | Pullan, Jack, illustrator.
Title: Help for Dear Dragon / by Margaret Hillert ; illustrated by Jack Pullan.
Description: Chicago, IL : Norwood House Press, [2016] | Series: A
  beginning-to-read book | Summary: "A boy gets help for his sick dragon.
  With the assistance of a friendly veterinarian, Dear Dragon feels better
  and is able to play again. Completely re-illustrated from original
  edition. Includes reading activities and a word list"-- Provided by
  publisher.
Identifiers: LCCN 2015046736 (print) | LCCN 2016014724 (ebook) | ISBN
  9781599537696 (library edition : alk. paper) | ISBN 9781603578950 (eBook)
Subjects: | CYAC: Veterinarians--Fiction. | Dragons--Fiction.
Classification: LCC PZ7.H558 He 2016 (print) | LCC PZ7.H558 (ebook) | DDC
  [E]--dc23
LC record available at http://lccn.loc.gov/2015046736

-072016
Manufactured in the United States of America in North Mankato, Minnesota.

Here you are.
Here is something to eat.
It is what you like.

No?
You do not want it?
That is funny.

You did not want to get up.
Now you do not want to eat.
You do not look good.
What is it?
What can I do?

You are not happy.
I am not happy.
This is not good.
I have to get help for you.

Come on.
Get in here.
We will go for help.

Away we go.
This way.
This way.
You will see.

Here it is.
This is where we want to go.
In here.
In here.

PET DOCTOR
DR. LEE
D.V.M.

Oh, my.
Look here—
and here—
and here.

Have you come
to get help, too?
This is a good spot for it.

Come in.
Come in.
Jump up here.
I want to have a look at you.

I will look down here
to see what I can see.

My, you do not look too good.
Not too good.
But, I can help.

I want to look at this, too.
I want to find out something
with this.

Now I will do this.
This will be
a big help to you.

Yes, yes.
This is good for you.
And you are a good
little dragon.

Here is something red.
I want you to have this, too.
It is something that will help.

Now you can get down.
Down —
down —
down.

And away you go.
You will want to eat now.
You will want to run and play.

Come on.
Come on.
Run, run, run!
I will get you
something good to eat.

Here you are.
Eat it up, and we will
go out to play.

What fun we will have!

DRAGON
FOOD

Here you are with me.
And here I am with you.
Now it is a happy day,
Dear Dragon.

The following activities support the findings of the National Reading Panel that determined the most effective components for reading instruction are: Phonemic Awareness, Phonics, Vocabulary, Fluency, and Text Comprehension.

Phonemic Awareness: The /h/ sound

Deletion: Ask your child to say the following words without the beginning /**h**/ sound:

hat - /h/ = at	hop - /h/ = op	ham - /h/ = am
hit - /h/ = it	his - /h/ = is	harm - /h/ = arm
hand - /h/ = and	hair - /h/ = air	

Phonics: The letter Hh

1. Demonstrate how to form the letters **H** and **h** for your child.

2. Have your child practice writing **H** and **h** at least three times each.

3. Ask your child to point to the words in the book that start with the letter **h**.

4. Write down the following words and ask your child to circle the letter **h** in each word:

happy	hand	mother	hug
help	father	home	how
hair	the	there	here
hut	house	where	have

Vocabulary: Be the Words

1. Write the following words on separate pieces of paper:

cough	cold	stomach ache
sore throat	sneeze	fever

2. Say each word and ask your child to act it out.

3. Act out each word and ask your child to point to the correct word(s).

Fluency: Choral Reading

1. Reread the story to your child at least two more times while your child tracks the print by running a finger under the words as they are read. Ask your child to read the words he or she knows with you.

2. Reread the story aloud together. Be careful to read at a rate that your child can keep up with.

3. Repeat choral reading and allow your child to be the lead reader and ask him or her to change from a whisper to a loud voice while you follow along and change your voice.

Text Comprehension: Discussion Time

1. Ask your child to retell the sequence of events in the story.

2. To check comprehension, ask your child the following questions:

   • Where did the boy take Dear Dragon?

   • How did the boy know Dear Dragon needed help?

   • Describe a time when you were sick. Who helped you and how?

WORD LIST

Help for Dear Dragon uses the 65 words listed below.

This list can be used to practice reading the words that appear in the text. You may wish to write the words on index cards and use them to help your child build automatic word recognition. Regular practice with these words will enhance your child's fluency in reading connected text.

a	day	happy	no	that
am	dear	have	not	this
and	did	help	now	to
are	do	here		too
at	down		oh	
away	dragon	I	on	up
		in	out	
be	eat	is		want
big		it	play	way
but	find			we
	for	jump	red	what
can	fun		run	where
come	funny	like		will
		little	see	with
	get	look	something	
	go		spot	yes
	good	me		you
		my		

ABOUT THE AUTHOR Margaret Hillert has helped millions of children all over the world learn to read independently. She was a first grade teacher for 34 years and during that time started writing books that her students could both gain confidence in reading and enjoy. She wrote well over 100 books for children just learning to read. As a child, she enjoyed writing poetry and continued her poetic writings as an adult for both children and adults.

Photograph by Glenna Washburn

ABOUT THE ILLUSTRATOR A talented and creative illustrator, Jack Pullan, is a graduate of William Jewell College. He has also studied informally at Oxford University and the Kansas City Art Institute. He was mentored by the renowned watercolor artists, Jim Hamil and Bill Amend. Jack's work has graced the pages of many enjoyable children's books, various educational materials, cartoon strips, as well as many greeting cards. Jack currently resides in Kansas.